the Peterkins' Christmas

Adapted by Elizabeth Spurr

from the original story by
Lucretia P. Hale

Illustrated by Wendy Anderson Halperin

ATHENEUM BOOKS FOR YOUNG READERS   New York   London   Toronto   Sydney

The Peterkins lived a long time ago,

in the horse-and-buggy days. Families then were much the same as families now—sometimes somber and serious, often senseless and silly.

Mr. and Mrs. Peterkin had six children: Agamemnon, Solomon John, and Elizabeth Eliza, plus three younger sons who, because they forgot to name them, were called the Little Boys. The Peterkins also had a nameless friend known only as the Lady from Philadelphia, whose wisdom and kindness often saved the family from disaster when their silliness got out of hand.

> *Dear Lady from Philadelphia,*
>
> *We so missed you during the Christmas season. But you must realize that you were very much a part of our Yuletide— and not just in spirit!*
>
> *Let me recount to you the holiday happenings, which (as is often the case with celebrations) included a few mishaps.*

Although still sweltering through the dog days of September, the Peterkins felt it was none too soon to plan their Christmas festivities. So after the Little Boys had trotted off to school, the three older children conferred with their parents at the round oak breakfast table.

To begin with, we planned the tree, which was to be, as usual, a wondrous surprise, which meant we should take great pains for secrecy.

Mr. Peterkin adjusted his pince-nez. "We must, as always, have a tree this year. Which means we must proceed with the greatest secrecy."

"We will want to surprise the neighbors as well as our family," said Agamemnon.

"Won't the Little Boys be thrilled?" said Elizabeth Eliza. "They will jump right out of their india-rubber boots!"

Mrs. Peterkin poured salt instead of sugar into her coffee, which she sometimes did when excited. "We must be extremely careful not to let on." She tasted her coffee and frowned, but went on talking. "Last year everyone suspected."

"And each year before that," said Solomon John.

"I have an idea," said Agamemnon. "We shall never mention the word 'tree' aloud. We will call it the You-Know-What."

So Mr. Peterkin went off to Mr. Bromwick's wood lot to select the You-Know-What. He paced through acres of trees until he found just the right specimen—green and full and even.

"I will tag it for you," said Mr. Bromwick.

"Please, no. This You-Know-What is a surprise. No one must see my name on it."

"Then how will you find it again?"

Mr. Peterkin thought for a moment. "I have it: I will spell my name backward:

One by one the Peterkins snuck out, at sunrise or by lantern light, to admire the You-Know-What, which was not hard to find, since, with the first frost yet to come, it was the only tree with a tag.

The Little Boys began taking long walks, to see the new pumpkins, they said, or to gather leaves for the Thanksgiving table. They came home whistling "Jingle Bells," or giggling about Nikretep, but did not breathe a word about what they now knew.

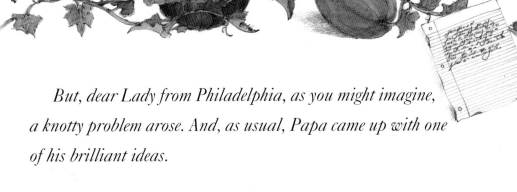

But, dear Lady from Philadelphia, as you might imagine, a knotty problem arose. And, as usual, Papa came up with one of his brilliant ideas.

A few weeks before Christmas Mr. Peterkin had the You-Know-What cut down and brought secretly into neighbor Larkins' barn. He measured it top to bottom. "Oh, no!"

He measured again, bottom to top. "It can't be!"

The tree was too high to stand in the back parlor.

Mr. Peterkin called Mrs. Peterkin, Agamemnon, and Elizabeth Eliza to a meeting in the back parlor, with the doors locked and the drapes drawn.

"Whatever shall we do about the You-Know-What?" wailed Mrs. Peterkin, fussing with her ruffled fichu.

All turned to Agamemnon. (Because he had had a year of college, the family valued his ideas.) "Why not set it up slanting?" he suggested.

"Oh, dear no!" said Mrs. Peterkin. "That would make me quite dizzy. Besides, the candles would drip, and perhaps set the house on fire."

"I have a better idea," said Mr. Peterkin. "We can raise the parlor ceiling."

"But, Father," said Elizabeth Eliza, "my bedroom is right above. If you raise the floor, I will bump my head on my ceiling, which might cause me to lose my wits."

It was decided that they would alter only the back part of the parlor, creating a ridge across the end of Elizabeth Eliza's room.

"Excellent idea," said Mrs. Peterkin. "It will cut right through the worn place in Elizabeth Eliza's carpet."

Elizabeth Eliza agreed. She would love a new carpet.

So we called the carpenter to raise the ceiling. There followed a terrible din, which did not suit Mama's frail disposition, nor mine, if the truth were known. But one must learn to take life's little bumps.

When the carpenter came, he was shocked at the Peterkins' plan. "Why don't I just cut off the bottom of the tree?"

"You mean the You-Know-What," whispered Mr. Peterkin.

"No, I don't know what," said the carpenter, shrugging.

"We must proceed as planned," said Elizabeth Eliza. "I've already cut away my carpet."

"I like my idea of a higher ceiling," said Mr. Peterkin. "Next year's You-Know-What might again grow too tall."

The folding doors to the back parlor were closed. *Bang! Clunk! Clatter!* For nearly a fortnight the carpenter created a great rain of falling plaster and a litter of wood chips and shavings.

Mrs. Peterkin stood by with her feather duster, trying to tidy up, but the noise gave her a headache and she took to her bed.

The Little Boys were delighted with all the disturbance. They came to Elizabeth Eliza in the kitchen. "What is all that racket?"

Elizabeth Eliza began rattling pots and pans. She turned to Amanda, the cook. "Do you hear anything?"

Amanda chopped her vegetables with a fury. "No, I don't hear a thing."

Upstairs a wide hole appeared in Elizabeth Eliza's room. She called her parents to take a look. "I'm dreadfully afraid I might fall through."

"No problem," said Mr. Peterkin. "We can string a rope across the opening. And we'll tie on bells in case you walk in your sleep."

"I have a better idea," said Mrs. Peterkin. "We can move Elizabeth Eliza's bed into the back parlor. Then if she falls, she will fall into bed!"

"I don't even like falling asleep," said Elizabeth Eliza.

In a huff she packed her overnight bag and stayed at the Bromwicks' until the hole was covered.

On her return home Elizabeth Eliza found that the "hump" in her bedroom had turned out higher than expected. She covered it with pieces of her old carpet and tossed flowered pillows at each end to make it look like a divan (albeit a very high one).

"Ah, just the spot to cozy up with my novel." But as she stretched out—*thump*—her head hit the ceiling.

The next day with liniment and adhesive on her brow, she nailed padding to the ceiling.

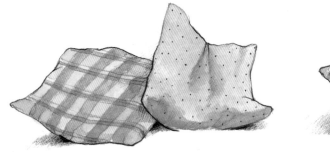

While the work was being completed in the parlor, I made several trips into town to buy trimmings for the tree. But each time, for one reason or another (perhaps my bumped head), I was distracted. So I was much relieved to find that Solomon John and the Little Boys had made plans themselves.

Elizabeth Eliza went into town to buy trimmings for the tree. But
she dallied in the shops so long—oh, the petticoats and bustles, oh,
the hats with birds!—that she quite forgot what she had come for.

On another trip she dropped by the Ice House for ice, which she and Amanda planned to mix with cream to make ice cream. At the candle shop, as she pondered over stars and crystal drops, the ice dripped all over the floor. She hurried home with an empty, wet satchel.

Solomon John called the Little Boys to his room. "Can you keep a secret?" He showed them a bushel of bayberries from which he planned to make candles for the tree. Next he fetched a box of wood scraps that the carpenters had left, and handed the boys sheets of gold paper. "You can make gilt apples," he said.

"For the You-Know-What?" said the Little Boys, grinning.

Solomon John drew himself up tall. "Whoever said we were having a You-Know-What?"

When the carpenter's noise finally abated, I began practicing Christmas carols on my piano. However, there was one impediment, and once again the need for a brilliant Peterkin solution.

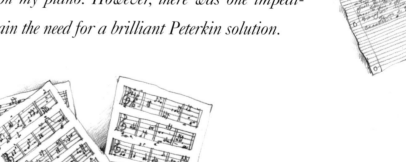

In mid-December, Elizabeth Eliza came downstairs with her
songbook to practice Christmas carols. But when she opened the
door of the rear parlor, she gasped. "Mama, come see! The carpenter
has moved the piano."

Mrs. Peterkin rustled in. "Yes, I know. The piano was standing
where the Christmas tree will be."

"But he faced it backside out. The keyboard faces the window!"

"I asked him to," said Mrs. Peterkin. "Otherwise the keys would
be covered with plaster dust."

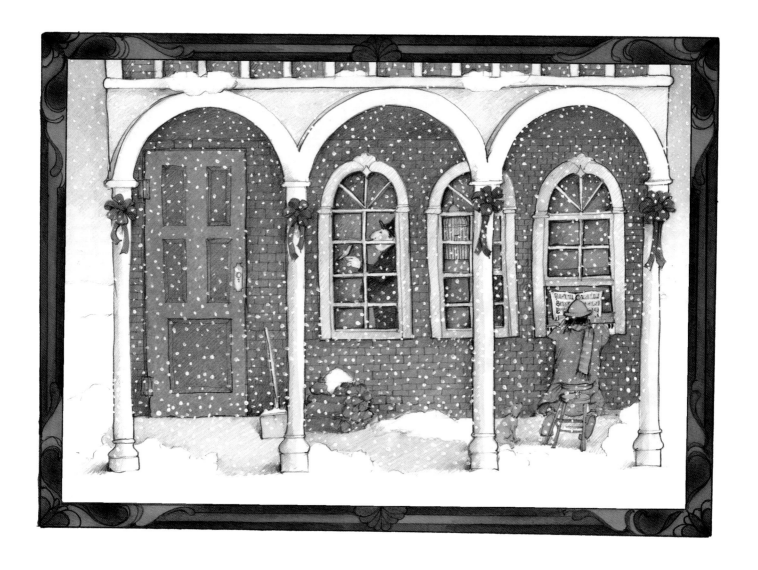

"We could have closed the lid."

Mrs. Peterkin adjusted the comb in her chignon. "There's no reason to fret. You can sit on the piazza and reach in through the window to practice."

Elizabeth Eliza's face broke into a smile. "Why, so I can. That way our neighbors can enjoy the music too."

So Elizabeth Eliza, in cloak and muffler, daily repaired to the piazza to play. She fancied that the notes sounded especially fresh and crisp.

Christmas Day was rapidly approaching, which meant the arrival of all our aunts and uncles and cousins. We couldn't wait to see their expressions when they saw our beautiful You-Know-What.

Christmas Eve became a frenzy of activity, but not all of it merry. In all the excitement it was difficult to keep one's senses.

The afternoon before Christmas, while Mrs. Peterkin settled the newly arrived aunts and uncles and cousins in the front room, Mr. Peterkin called Elizabeth Eliza and Solomon John to a private meeting in the back parlor. The tree stood on a box, stretching into its special space.

"So green, so full, so even," said Mr. Peterkin.

Solomon John rolled his eyes. "And so tall!"

"We'll need a carload of pretty things," Elizabeth Eliza said, sighing, "to deck it properly."

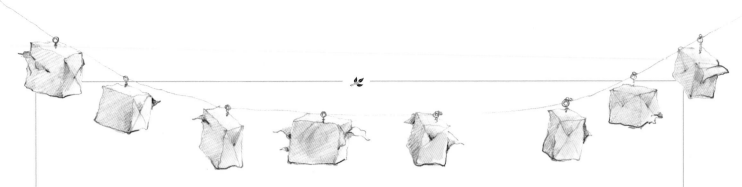

Solomon John brought in his supply of candles, which had turned out small and stringy, and very few at that.

"This is all?" moaned Elizabeth Eliza.

"A bushel of bayberries," complained her brother, "does not produce much wax."

On the lower branches he hung the gilt apples made by the Little Boys. "But they're so flat and square," said Mr. Peterkin.

Elizabeth Eliza frowned. "They don't look a bit like apples."

Solomon John lit a candle. It sputtered and went out.

The glorious You-Know-What looked like a secret that should have remained one.

"Can't someone take a train into town," asked Solomon John, "to buy gilt ornaments and candles? Can't we make caramels or sugarplums? String popcorn and cranberries?"

"I promised to help wrap the gifts," said Mr. Peterkin. "If we can remember where we hid them."

"I must help Amanda with Christmas dinner," said Elizabeth Eliza. "There's still the goose to pluck."

"Provided I can catch her," said Solomon John.

The situation looked grim. Christmas with an untrimmed tree and a house full of relatives. And then you may guess what happened. Talk about surprises!

Mr. Peterkin, Solomon John, and Elizabeth Eliza returned to their guests, forcing smiles to cover their dismay. A moment later came a loud knocking. The Little Boys, uncles, aunts, and cousins stared at the door. Who could be calling on Christmas Eve uninvited?

When the door was opened, they saw a plump, bearded man covered with snowflakes. At his feet was a large wooden crate.

"Santa Claus?" whispered the Little Boys.

The box was addressed to Elizabeth Eliza. "Ah yes," Mrs. Peterkin whispered to her daughter. "This must be your Christmas purchases. It's about time."

"But, Mama . . ."

Mrs. Peterkin ordered the box carried to the back parlor, as if nothing had happened.

In the back parlor Mr. Peterkin lighted the gas lamps while Solomon John took a hammer to the lid of the box.

Mrs. Peterkin turned to Elizabeth Eliza. "What a lot of shopping you did."

"Yes. But I'm afraid that . . ."

Solomon John pounded and tugged and wrenched and pried, till finally . . .

"Nooh!" he gasped.

"Ohhh!" cried Elizabeth Eliza.

"Land o' lovin'!" Mrs. Peterkin held her brow and retired to the velvet settee. "Daughter, what have you done?"

The inside of the box fairly glowed. It was filled with every kind of gilt hanging-thing, from golden pea pods to butterflies on springs.

"Flags and lanterns!" shouted Solomon John.

"Birds in cages!" said Elizabeth Eliza. "Birds on nests. A whole skyful of shining birds!"

"And here are some real gilt apples," said Mr. Peterkin. "And your candles."

At the bottom of the crate, Elizabeth Eliza found a tin of bonbons and a note from the Lady from Philadelphia:

I thought you could use these pretties for your Christmas tree.

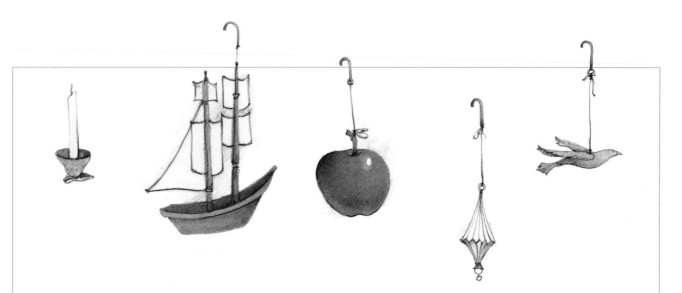

"How clever of her to guess," said Mrs. Peterkin, "that we would have a tree this year."

"Huzzah!" shouted Solomon John.

Elizabeth Eliza raised her eyes heavenward. "We are saved!"

The Little Boys and the cousins banged on the doors of the back parlor. "What's happening in there?"

When they saw the tree, the Little Boys almost jumped out of their india-rubber boots.

When Mr. Peterkin opened the doors, the children screamed with glee. "A You-Know-What! A Christmas tree!"

"So big!" said the Little Boys. "It even reaches the ceiling!"

"Come everyone," said Mrs. Peterkin to the family and the aunts and uncles and cousins. "Hang an ornament and make a wish."

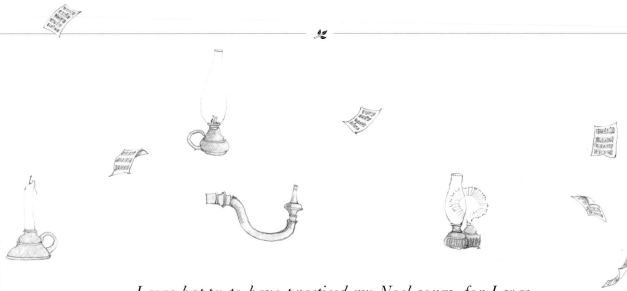

I was happy to have practiced my Noel songs, for I was, indeed, called upon to perform. My playing, however, got a somewhat chilly reception.

"Now we must sing some carols," said Mr. Peterkin.

Elizabeth Eliza opened the window, then donned her cape and scarf and went out to the piazza. Strains of "Silent Night" tinkled through the air. But what followed was far from silent. A sudden blast of north wind filled the parlor with snow flurries, blowing out the lamps and candles and leaving the Peterkins in damp, chilly darkness.

On the porch Elizabeth Eliza, shivering against the icy blasts, kept on at the piano. The wind blew away her songbook, but she now knew the notes by heart.

As she paused to phrase, someone inside the parlor slammed down the window.

Oh, dear, thought Elizabeth Eliza. *Don't they like my playing?*

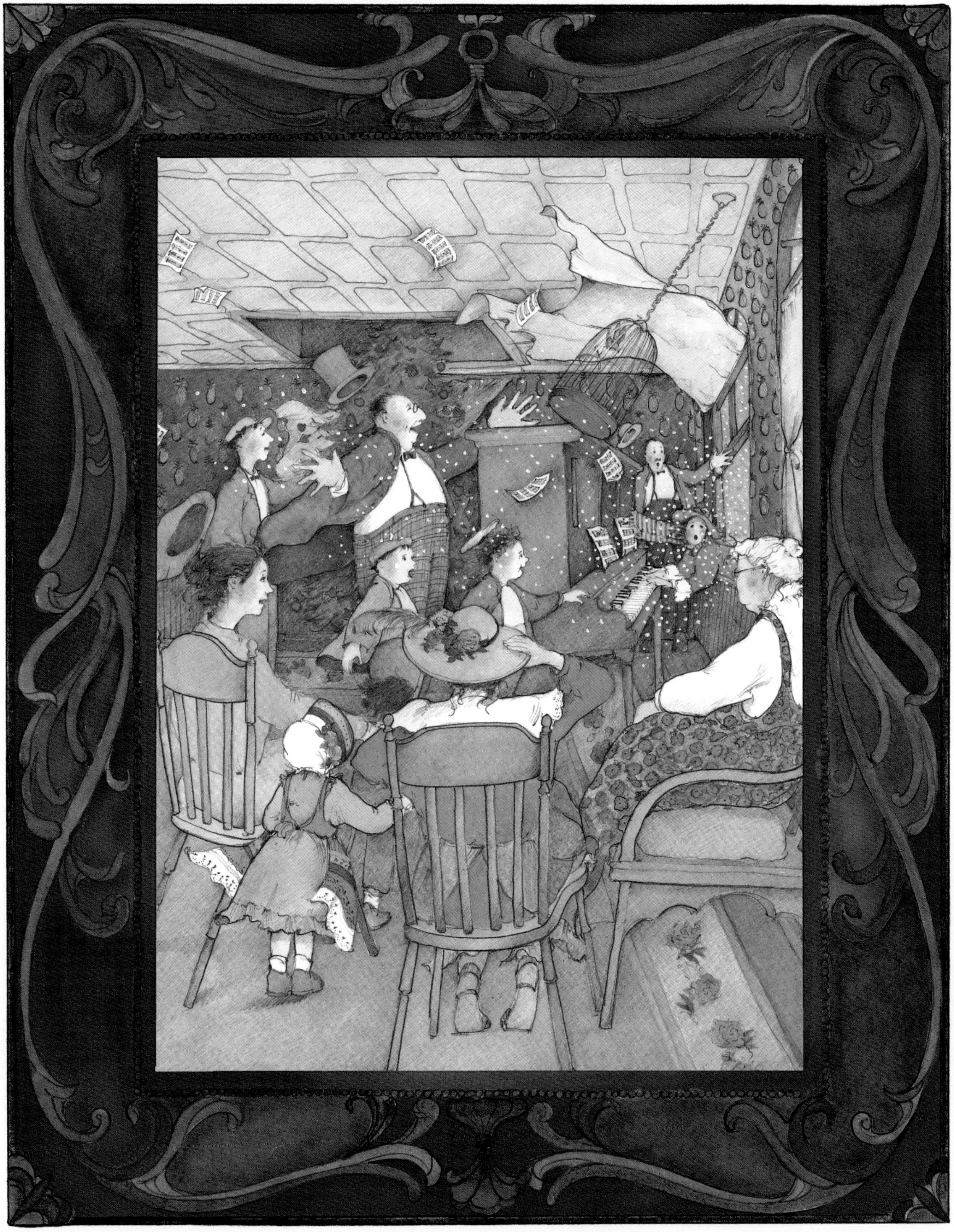

When the fires had been stoked and the lamps and candles relit, Mr. Peterkin remarked to the family and aunts and uncles and cousins, "It appears a heavy storm is coming. Perhaps we should invite the neighbors in to see our tree right away."

Elizabeth Eliza sipped her hot lemonade. "Wouldn't it be lovely if we all got snowed in together? I do so enjoy having Christmas company."

And so, dear Lady from Philadelphia, we invited all the neighbors for Christmas Eve. How astounded they were to see our magnificent tree!

I must now go pluck the goose (if she has been caught), but I did want to thank you and yours for making our Christmas the most splendid ever.

Sincerely yours,
Elizabeth Eliza Peterkin

For Howard, who introduced me to the Peterkins
—E. S.

To all the readers in the Upper Peninsula of Michigan
—W. A. H.

Atheneum Books for Young Readers
An imprint of Simon & Schuster Children's Publishing Division
1230 Avenue of the Americas
New York, New York 10020

Book design by Sonia Chaghatzbanian
The text of this book is set in Caslon.
The illustrations are rendered in watercolors.

Manufactured in China
First Edition

2 4 6 8 10 9 7 5 3 1
Library of Congress Cataloging-in-Publication Data
Spurr, Elizabeth.
The Peterkins' Christmas / by Lucretia P. Hale ; adapted by Elizabeth Spurr ;
illustrated by Wendy Anderson Halperin.
p.   cm.
Adaptation of one episode from the Peterkin papers.
Summary: Their usual silliness reigns as the eccentric Peterkin family prepares for Christmas.
ISBN 0-689-83023-8
[1. Christmas—Fiction. 2. Family life—Fiction. 3. Humorous stories.]
I. Hale, Lucretia P. (Lucretia Peabody), 1820–1900. Peterkin papers. II. Halperin, Wendy Anderson, ill.
III. Title.
PZ7.S7695 Pe 2003
[Fic]—dc21   00-069981